Let's Play Basketball

Gloria Santos

illustrated by
Joel Gennari

PowerKiDS
press.

New York

Published in 2018 by The Rosen Publishing Group, Inc.
29 East 21st Street, New York, NY 10010

First Edition

Managing Editor: Nathalie Beullens-Maoui
Editor: Melissa Raé Shofner
Art Director: Michael Flynn
Book Design: Raúl Rodriguez
Illustrator: Joel Gennari

Cataloging-in-Publication Data

Names: Santos, Gloria, author.
Title: Let's play basketball / Gloria Santos.
Description: New York : PowerKids Press, [2018] | Series: Let's get active! |
  Includes index.
Identifiers: LCCN 2017013190| ISBN 9781538327371 (pbk. book) | ISBN
  9781538327685 (6 pack) | ISBN 9781508163879 (library bound book)
Subjects: LCSH: Basketball–Juvenile literature.
Classification: LCC GV885.1 .S268 2018 | DDC 796.323–dc23
LC record available at https://lccn.loc.gov/2017013190

Manufactured in the United States of America

CPSIA Compliance Information: Batch #BW18PK. For further information contact Rosen Publishing, New York, New York at 1-800-237-9932

Contents

I Love Basketball   4

Warming Up   8

Passing and Shooting   12

In the Hoop   18

Words to Know   24

Index   24

I like to play basketball.
It's my favorite sport.

Mom and I go to the park
with my friends.

We play basketball on the court.

We do stretches to warm up.

We pass the ball around in a circle.

Liza and Cory want to play a game. Trey will be on my team.

I pass the basketball to Trey.

He bounces the ball up and down.

Trey shoots the basketball.

It hits the hoop and bounces off.

Cory catches the ball.

He races across the court in
his wheelchair.

Liza is all alone under the hoop.

She waves to Cory for the ball.

Liza takes the shot.

The basketball goes in the hoop!
That's two points!

Basketball is so much fun! I love
to play basketball with my friends!

Words to Know

court

hoop

wheelchair

Index

C
court, 7, 17

H
hoop, 15, 18, 21

P
pass, 9, 12

T
team, 11